zap

zap

PAUL FLEISCHMAN

CANDLEWICK PRESS
CAMBRIDGE, MASSACHUSETTS

For Saralee and all the Halprins

Copyright © 2005 by Paul Fleischman

If you are interested in staging a production of *Zap*, please send your written request to the Contracts and Rights Department, Candlewick Press, 2067 Massachusetts Avenue, Cambridge, MA 02140. Fax 617-661-0565

First paperback edition 2006

The Library of Congress has cataloged the hardcover edition as follows:

Fleischman, Paul.
Zap / Paul Fleischman —1st ed.
p.   cm.
ISBN-10 0-7636-2774-7 (hardcover)
ISBN-13 978-0-7636-2774-4 (hardcover)
1. Theater—Drama. 2. Young adult drama, American.   I. Title.
PS3556.L42268Z44   2005
812'.54—dc22   2005050790

ISBN-10 0-7636-3234-1 (paperback)
ISBN-13 978-0-7636-3234-2 (paperback)

2 4 6 8 10 9 7 5 3 1

Printed in the United States of America

This book was typeset in Galliard.
Book design by Michelle Gengaro-Kokmen

Candlewick Press
2067 Massachusetts Avenue
Cambridge, Massachusetts 02140

visit us at www.candlewick.com

Foreword

I was driving by a high school, saw the sign advertising *Grease,* and said out loud, "Again?"

Like Pepsi or Coke paying to be a school's sole soft drink, *Grease* and *Romeo and Juliet* had captured the drama departments. They and two or three other plays seemed to be in eternal rotation, like the seasons. Hadn't anything new been written in the past thirty years that would work on the high-school stage?

I decided to take my own challenge. Not that I'd ever acted in a play. My one tryout in high school had elicited nothing more from the drama teacher than the comment "You have a low voice." Nor had I ever written a bona fide play. I knew "Break a leg" but was vague about "downstage left." Perhaps my innocence shows in *Zap*'s technical challenges. Then again, without that daring, nothing would ever get written, in any genre.

For years, I'd been collecting ideas under the heading "Multiple Genres." Imagine the sound of pounding on Hamlet's castle door in Denmark, the guard opens up, and there stand two girls from Sweet Valley High, who proceed to turn tragedy into comedy. Time travel had been done over and over; my idea was cross-book travel. The problem was finding an explanation. The usual solutions—time machines, doors on the past—didn't appeal to me. Then my eye fell on the remote control. Rather than overlap genres, I could switch back and forth among them. This wasn't fantasy; it was taking place every night across the country. All I had to do was to bring it out of the living room and onto the stage. It would suit high schools, which like huge casts. They're also, I found, hungry for female roles. I obliged, and made the choicest role a female performance artist.

With the zapper in hand, I could stage a collision between not just two plays, but as many as an audience could keep straight. I settled on seven. Surely, I thought, one of them had to be by Shakespeare. I decided on *Richard III,* famed for its hunchbacked king and his final, frantic plea, "My kingdom for a horse!"—perhaps the most famous line in all of theater after "To be or not to be."

Rather than use six other real plays, I decided to write my own, modeled on the most familiar categories—drama's prime-time offerings. Thus, there's a mystery set in the English countryside during World War I, strongly reminiscent of Agatha Christie. Though she's most famous for her detective novels, she wrote plays as well, including the longest-running play of all time, *The Mousetrap,* in which a series of guests at an isolated inn are murdered.

I thought next of Anton Chekhov, Russia's greatest playwright, author of *The Cherry Orchard, Uncle Vanya,*

The Three Sisters. His brooding dramas are set in the late 1800s and peopled with once-proud families enfeebled by dreaming and scheming. Russian accents would contrast nicely with British accents. I put Chekhov in my shopping cart.

It struck me that Chekhov's characters would have felt at home in Tennessee Williams's plays set in the American South, plays similarly filled with vanished fortunes, twisted families, and sensitive characters who take refuge in drink and rail against the lack of culture in the countryside. *Cat on a Hot Tin Roof, The Glass Menagerie,* and *A Streetcar Named Desire* were all triumphs on the stage and later as movies. Dysfunctional southern families with a taste for liquor and eccentricity are still a staple of the stage and screen. I definitely needed a southern play.

What about comedy? The obvious model was Neil Simon, the comedy king of Broadway for decades, author of such smash hits as *The Odd Couple* and *The Sunshine Boys.* He's the master of the wisecrack, the Woody Allen of the theater, whose plays deal with family foibles and modern life as lived in New York.

Speaking of modern, what about a play along the lines of Samuel Beckett's *Waiting for Godot,* something avant-garde, full of non sequiturs, silences, and eerie situations of maddening hopelessness? The "theater of the absurd" grew out of the two world wars' incomprehensible slaughter and the loss of faith that life made any sense. Corpses, I noticed, often figured in these plays. I decided I'd find a place for a corpse or two in mine. Last, for something truly up-to-date,

I'd put in a monologue by a performance artist, one who spits on the traditions of the theater, unaware that she's repeating its ageless themes.

Every few years, after a string of serious books, I'm ready to pack my bags and kazoo and take a vacation to comedy. *Zap* was my latest trip. I had a ball writing it. The question facing me when I finished was whether it would actually work.

When I heard that nearby Pacific Grove High School in California wanted to give the premiere, I was elated. Kelly Cool, the aptly named director, invited me to be part of the whole process, giving me a fabulous education along the way. The audiences were enlightening as well. Novelists never see the reader who chuckles or underlines a passage; playwrights are right in the same room. When the crowd doesn't laugh where you wanted, you take note. When the room resounds, there's no better place to be. Subsequent productions by James Rayfield's students at Blake High School in Tampa, Florida, and at New York City's Stuyvesant High School, under the guidance of Annie Thoms, nudged me farther along the learning curve. It's been a thrill to watch the actors add inflections and gestures that weren't on the page. Gratitude and bouquets to all three casts, several of whose inventive touches I've incorporated into the text.

My thanks go as well to Walter Mayes, Ron McCutchan, and Dan Gotch for the gift of their time and advice. And, as ever, a special ovation for my incomparably insightful and dedicated editor, Marc Aronson.

Zap was given its first public performance November 1, 2002, at Pacific Grove High School in Pacific Grove, California, with the following cast:

EMMALINE GRAY . . . . Lauren Reppy
BEETON . . . . Natalie Melendez
COLONEL HARDWICKE . . . . Chris Deacon
MRS. MARJORIE HARDWICKE . . . . Guin Rojek
REVEREND SMYTHE . . . . Jessica Glen
LADY VANESSA DENSLOW . . . . Catlin Seavey
INSPECTOR SWIFT; BUCKINGHAM . . . . Tim Cool
CLIFFORD GRAY . . . . Elliot Rubin
IRV WEINSTEIN . . . . Tyler Shilstone
SAMMY . . . . Matt Cool
AUDREY MCPHERSON . . . . Jane Franklin
RICHARD III . . . . Ryan Kendall
LADY ANNE; PRINCE EDWARD . . . . Gwyneth Alldis
NORFOLK; KONSTANTIN . . . . Michael Brusuelas
NIKOLAI VOLNIKOV . . . . Nick Stiles
IRINA . . . . Megan Alldis
PAVEL . . . . Sean Muhl
OLGA . . . . Paige Dwyer
MARSHA . . . . Michelle Maddox
MAN . . . . Khalid Hussein
WOMAN . . . . Ashley Brewer
BELLBOY . . . . Whitney VanZwol
AARON PUCKETT . . . . Kenny Neely
REGINALD . . . . Will Cryer
CAROLINE . . . . Heather Seavey
LUKE . . . . Ben Middlebrook
GRANDMAMMY . . . . Sarah Booth-Olvera

Director . . . . Kelly Cool
Sound . . . . Dana Fleischman
Lighting Design . . . . Mark Stotzer
Lighting . . . . Scott Rudoni
Spotlight . . . . Patrick Cool
Set Artist . . . . Margie Anderson
Stage Crew . . . . Katie Miller, Whitney VanZwol

Characters

THE HOUSE MANAGER

The English Mystery
EMMALINE GRAY
CLIFFORD GRAY, her husband
BEETON, their butler
COLONEL HARDWICKE
MRS. MARJORIE
  HARDWICKE, his wife
REVEREND SMYTHE
LADY VANESSA DENSLOW
INSPECTOR SWIFT

The Comedy
IRV WEINSTEIN
SAMMY
AUDREY McPHERSON

Shakespeare's Richard III
Duke of GLOUCESTER,
  later King RICHARD III
LADY ANNE, later married to
  Richard
Duke of BUCKINGHAM
Duke of NORFOLK
PRINCE EDWARD, Richard's
  nephew

The Russian Play
NIKOLAI VOLNIKOV
IRINA, his wife
KONSTANTIN, his great-
  grandfather
PAVEL, his cousin
OLGA, his aunt

The Performance Art Monologue
MARSHA

The Avant-Garde Play
MAN
WOMAN

The Southern Play
AARON PUCKETT
REGINALD, his father
CAROLINE, his half sister
LUKE, his stepbrother
GRANDMAMMY

Production Notes

A single set is used throughout. Actors are in period costume. When switching from one play to another, a loud electronic sound is heard, followed by a brief blackout, during which the actors quickly enter and exit. The speed of these cast changes is key.

I highly recommend reading or seeing the works mentioned in the foreword or others in the genre. It's crucial to know the conventions that are colliding. It's just as important to remain true to them despite the growing chaos onstage. None of the laughter should be coming from the cast. The straighter it's played, the funnier it will be.

The image of a remote control could be copied onto programs as a nod to the play's conceit.

Making use of the following doubling possibilities reduces the cast requirements to 12 males and 8 females:

REGINALD with PAVEL
OLGA with MRS. HARDWICKE
HOUSE MANAGER with CLIFFORD GRAY and
   NORFOLK
INSPECTOR SWIFT with BUCKINGHAM and LUKE
AUDREY MCPHERSON with LADY ANNE and
   GRANDMAMMY
BEETON with PRINCE EDWARD and KONSTANTIN

The show runs roughly eighty-five minutes and should be presented without intermission.

zap

(Before curtain rises, the HOUSE MANAGER addresses the audience.)

HOUSE MANAGER. Good evening. Thank you all for coming to tonight's world premiere. A few preliminaries. No photographs, please, flash or otherwise. Likewise, no recording of any kind. Please check that all cell phones and pagers are turned off. Please do, however, make use of the remote controls you should have found on your seats. Vote for a change whenever you feel the need. The computer backstage will log all requests and make a switch when a sufficient threshold has been reached. Our aim is to please you, the audience. You, after all, are why we are here. To entertain *you* is our first and foremost duty. Why else would—

(Zap sound. Blackout. Curtain rises on a drawing room furnished in a mix of styles, from 1860 to 1960. A long couch and two chairs occupy the center of the room. There is an old black telephone atop a telephone table, a wastebasket, a bookcase, a fishbowl with goldfish, and a full whiskey bottle

and set of glasses. The fishbowl and whiskey bottle must be clearly visible to the audience.)

(Lights up on the ENGLISH MYSTERY. The year is 1916, the place an estate in the English countryside. Distant thunder is heard. EMMALINE GRAY, thirty and distraught, enters scanning a guest list and stops BEETON, passing in the other direction. Actors use English accents.)

EMMALINE. Beeton—there you are. Any word from the station?

BEETON. The train is expected on time, madam. Unless the bridge at Highstoke were to be washed out.

EMMALINE. I pray it shan't be. He only has five days' leave. Everything must be perfect for him. You spoke to the cook?

BEETON. Yes, madam. Roast beef shall be served. And English peas.

EMMALINE. Nothing French on the menu whatsoever, does she understand?

BEETON. Yes, madam. Fear not.

EMMALINE. Nothing that might possibly remind him of the fighting. His last letter has me quite . . .

(She trails off, then looks at the guest list.)

Oh, Beeton. There's been an addition to the guest list. I've invited Inspector Swift up from London. I'm hoping he'll enthrall us with his latest case and take all our minds off this wretched war—especially Clifford's.

BEETON. I shall see that the table is set for seven.

(He begins to leave.)

EMMALINE. Oh, and Beeton. Tell the entire staff to be on special guard against dropped pots and slammed doors and such. We must spare him loud noises of any sort.

BEETON. Certainly, madam.

(He begins to leave, getting farther this time.)

EMMALINE. And Beeton. Nothing red on the menu. Blood-red and runny. You understand.

BEETON. I shall speak to the cook about the brandied cherries, madam.

(He exits.)

EMMALINE. Oh, and Beeton—

(Zap sound. Blackout. Lights come up on the COMEDY. The time is summer, 1965, the place New York City. SAMMY, thirty, is lying on the couch and scanning the sports page, paying more attention to it than to IRV, forty-five, who's reading aloud from the New York Times while striding about the room. Both speak with New York accents.)

IRV. *(With heavy mockery.)* "Never before have the traumas and textures of modern life been rendered so unforgettably."

SAMMY. Uh-huh.

IRV. "The big, boisterous Bromberg family leaps into life off the page and takes up immediate residence in our hearts."

SAMMY. Uh-huh.

IRV. "The author's powers of invention astound. Equal parts comedy and tragedy, the book solves as well our foremost literary mystery—namely, when will the great American novel appear? The answer is 'Now.' Its name is *Brooklyn Blues*."

(He looks for a reaction from SAMMY, who finally glances up.)

SAMMY. Hey, that's great, Irv.

IRV. *(Exploding.)* What do you mean that's great! It's not my book!

SAMMY. Oh.

IRV. I mean it is mine! That's the whole point!

SAMMY. Right. Great. And in the *Times*. That's big. I mean it. Congratulations.

IRV. For what? His name's on it!

SAMMY. But I thought you said—

IRV. Jesus, will you listen? *(IRV collapses in a chair, then collects himself. Polka music sounds softly from below. IRV glares at the floor and stamps his foot, to no effect, sighs, and sits back.)* Max writes novels, I write novels. It's lonely. You're a sportswriter—you wouldn't know. You got forty thousand people around you at Yankee Stadium. All I've got is a crazy neighbor who listens to polka records. *(He pounds his feet more forcefully, then finally jumps up and down on the floor. The music stops.)* Maybe fifteen years ago, Max and I started having breakfast together. Once a week at Krupfeld's, on Thirty-fifth. We'd talk writing. Should he kill off a character, should I kill my agent, that kind of stuff. When Doris walked out and I was practically living at Krupfeld's, he let me talk it out hour after hour, for weeks. For months. Not just about Doris, but my parents, growing up, everything. That corner booth was like a couch at a shrink's.

SAMMY. You got a couch here. And you got me to listen, just two apartments down the hall. I'm a lot cheaper than a shrink.

IRV. Probably because you wouldn't know a cerebellum from a softball. Anyway, the last couple years, he said he had writer's block. Fine. Said he was thinking about quitting writing. Fine. Stopped showing up at Krupfeld's. Fine. And then, bam—*Brooklyn Blues*. I open it up, and it's my family, exactly! My rabbi father, my closet atheist of a mother, my meshuggah aunts, my brothers, the neighbors. All of 'em, including me! He stole my life when I wasn't looking! *(He swats at a fly with his newspaper and misses.)* So now Max McPherson is the great American author. Eating eggs Benedict at the Algonquin instead of dunking a doughnut in his coffee at Krupfeld's. While me, I'm living on Campbell's soup out of the can till the next piddling royalty check crawls up the stairs. And pouring my heart out to you, the only shrink I know who hogs the couch!

(He swats SAMMY's feet off the couch with the newspaper.)

SAMMY. Didn't he even change anything?

IRV. Oh, sure. Him with his "astounding powers of invention." Instead of allergies, he gave me bladder problems—the louse. And my father, he came from Minsk instead of Pinsk.

SAMMY. Wow. Isn't that paganism?

6

IRV. *(Rolls his eyes.)* No—and it's not *plagiarism* either. That's stealing someone's writing, which is against the law. Stealing somebody's actual family—that's legal!

SAMMY. A writer's family—man, that's his capital. That oughta be a crime.

IRV. You're exactly right.

SAMMY. So what are you gonna do?

IRV. I'm gonna see justice is done.

SAMMY. But you said—

IRV. Not legal justice. Legal is out. So we go to our back-up. Poetic justice.

SAMMY. He wrote poems about 'em too?

IRV. Poetic justice! He stole something from me, something beyond price. Now I steal from him. Which is where you come in, Sammy.

SAMMY. Steal? Steal what?

IRV. Don't worry. We're not jumping through a window and running out with the color TV.

SAMMY. So?

IRV. We need something more precious than that. Something that'll really hurt.

SAMMY. *(Pause.)* His typewriter?

IRV. More precious.

SAMMY. His car?

IRV. Keep going.

SAMMY. His . . . His . . . His—

IRV. *(Leans toward him.)* His wife. *(He swats at the fly, gets it, and grins at it.)* And it's gonna be sweet.

SAMMY. Jesus, Irv. Kidnapping? You could wind up in Sing Sing.

IRV. Yeah, and I hear they're looking for a sportswriter there to cover the knife fights. We're not going to kidnap her, you numbskull! We're going steal her affections. From him, to me. An eye for an eye, a theft for a theft. A betrayal for a betrayal. That's poetic justice.

(IRV throws down the newspaper, then feeds the fish in the fishbowl.)

SAMMY. But I thought you gave up on dames after Doris. Traded in females for fish.

IRV. Well, I'm making an exception. Not permanent. A temporary exception. Very temporary. Just long enough for Max to find out. And to rub his face in it. And you, with girls trooping in and out of your place like the dressing room at Bloomingdale's, you can be my coach. 'Cause it's been a while since I played this game.

SAMMY. *(He stands and sizes up IRV.)* Jeez, Irv. I don't know.

IRV. What do you mean you don't know! I'll use a fake name, so she won't know who I am. She's never met me, so she won't know my face. I'm not that bad looking. It's perfect!

SAMMY. It's not perfect! It's a long shot. It's the Cubs winning the World Series.

IRV. Thanks.

SAMMY. *(He walks around IRV, examining him, then checks his bicep. Pause.)* Can you kiss?

IRV. What—you're gonna send me down to the minors to brush up my skills? Of course I can kiss!

SAMMY. I'll bet. You and the Tin Man.

IRV. So it's been a while! So we squirt a little lubricating oil on my mouth.

SAMMY. And we know how dames go for the taste of 3-in-One. *(Pause.)* You dance?

IRV. Sure I dance. *(Searches his memory.)* Foxtrot . . . waltz . . .

SAMMY. . . . minuet. Irv, it's 1965! Maybe we oughta go for the color TV.

IRV. I can do it!

SAMMY. I'm just warning you, it might not be easy. Tell you what. Give me everything you know about her. Then I'll think about it for a couple of days and try to come up with a plan. But right now, I got my mind on other things. *(He checks his watch.)* Like the Yankees–Red Sox game in an hour. So if you don't mind—

(Zap sound. Blackout. Lights come up on the ENGLISH MYSTERY. BEETON is pouring glasses of whiskey, the bottle three-fourths empty by the time the drinks are all poured. EMMALINE enters with COL. and MRS. HARDWICKE, in their sixties, the fresh-faced REV. SMYTHE, and LADY DENSLOW, thirty and sultry.)

EMMALINE. His train's still not arrived. This awful storm—

(BEETON circulates with the drinks on a tray, exiting when the tray is empty.)

COL. HARDWICKE. From our English climate, one could conclude, Reverend, that God quite enjoys playing with water.

LADY DENSLOW. And playing with soldiers. Another boyish pastime.

EMMALINE. Only they're real, not toys. But I mustn't start. We're here to help Clifford forget all that.

LADY DENSLOW. *(Raising her glass.)* To forgetfulness!

THE OTHERS. To forgetfulness!

INSPECTOR SWIFT. *(Entering, dapper in evening clothes.)* The same toast apparently drunk by the witnesses on my last murder case.

EMMALINE. Inspector Swift! I'm so pleased you're here. Let me introduce you. Colonel and Mrs. Hardwicke, our nearest neighbors . . .

INSPECTOR SWIFT. I couldn't help noticing, motoring here, the extreme isolation of the houses.

COL. HARDWICKE. Makes us value human contact all the more.

(He chuckles nervously.)

INSPECTOR SWIFT. Indeed.

EMMALINE. Lady Vanessa Denslow. Her husband is also leading a regiment in France.

LADY DENSLOW. And will be dining this evening on horsemeat and rainwater.

INSPECTOR SWIFT. A most commendable sacrifice.

LADY DENSLOW. If we are what we eat, I suppose I should expect him to return even more of a beast than before.

EMMALINE. Reverend Smythe.

REV. SMYTHE. My apologies on the weather.

INSPECTOR SWIFT. Now, now. I don't think we'll be charging you as an accessory.

COL. HARDWICKE. A bit of a thorny question, what? Who *is* to blame for the weather? Perhaps that's the perfect crime, eh, Inspector?

(Chuckles nervously at his own observation.)

INSPECTOR SWIFT. Actually, I'm drawn to a different

question—namely, whether your nervous laugh is a regular habit or especially in my honor. *(Pause. He turns toward REV. SMYTHE.)* Odd how my presence, like yours, Reverend, leads many to anxious recollection of their sins. We are walking confession booths, you and I. Mr. Freud has dealt with the topic in fascinating detail, inquiring as to— please stop me if I'm boring you.

(The others all encourage INSPECTOR SWIFT to continue, with "Not at all," "Please go on," etc.)

INSPECTOR SWIFT. Very well. He began by—

(Zap sound. Blackout. Lights come up on RICHARD III, act 1, scene 1. GLOUCESTER, hunchbacked, stands alone. The actor portraying him delivers his lines with great pride in Shakespearean oratory.)

GLOUCESTER. Now is the winter of our discontent
Made glorious summer by this sun of York;
And all the clouds that lowr'd upon our house
In the deep bosom of the ocean buried.
Now are our brows—

(Zap sound. GLOUCESTER appears stunned. Blackout. Lights come up on the PERFORMANCE ART MONO-LOGUE. The time is the present. MARSHA, twenty-two, is dressed in black, from her motorcycle boots to her lipstick. She wears a bandanna on her head. She stumbles onstage

in slight confusion and flops onto the couch. She addresses the audience directly throughout.)

MARSHA. Whoa. This is too weird. Totally. I can't believe we're really doing this. And that I'm in it. That we all are. And with barely rehearsing, so we could hurry up and open and bring in some money. Talk about opening-night jitters. You should see it backstage. Bunch of chickens with their freaking heads cut off. And the director—totally ballistic. Not that that's exactly a change of pace. And Ron Throckmorton, the guy who runs the company, he's like oozing around telling everybody, "It's just for a little while, to help balance the books." Except we're always short of cash, even with none of us getting paid. And we're always about to lose our lease on the building, like right now, which is always gonna be the way it is in theater as long as people can sit at home and watch three million freaking cable channels with the zapper in one hand and a bowl of bubble gum fudge swirl in the other. But you gotta compete. Which is how Ron thought up putting on seven plays at once, something for everybody, including my performance art piece, and giving you guys zappers. High art meets short attention span. Naturally, I came down with a cold two days before we open, but who cares, you know? Acting's not actually my thing. Telling the truth is my thing. The whole truth. Nothing but the truth. The truth shall make you free! Somebody famous said that. *(She sniffles loudly and wipes her nose on her sleeve.)* The truth shall gross you out! I said that. *(She displays her sleeve to the audience.)* 'Cause I'm going to tell you about my repulsive family and my amazingly disgusting hometown and how I discovered theater and dared to tell the truth and how for the past five years I wouldn't stop telling the truth no matter what anybody—

(Zap sound. Blackout. Lights come up on the RUSSIAN PLAY. The time is 1870, a morning in spring. The place is a Russian country estate, home to the Volnikov family. NIKOLAI, thirty-five, rushes in and looks about in rapture. Actors use Russian accents.)

NIKOLAI. The sofa . . . Great-grandfather's books . . . the view of the birches! *(Calling offstage.)* Irina! We're here! *(To himself.)* Everything just as I recall it from my boyhood! Exactly! *(IRINA enters, thirty and beautiful, sulkily surveying the room's furnishings.)* Darling Irina! Can you believe it? Never again the noise of St. Petersburg, the crowding, the greed and moneygrubbing, the filthy air, the coarseness of spirit. Here in the country we shall both be reborn!

IRINA. *(Trailing a finger on the furniture and staring at her dusty fingertip.)* If that filthy ogre who brought our bags is our midwife, I believe I'd prefer a St. Petersburg specialist.

NIKOLAI. Dearest—you'll come to adore Gregor. Believe me.

IRINA. And frankly, Nikolai, I must confess that I feel no great need to be reborn. I leave that to the Hindus of India.

NIKOLAI. Come now, Irina. We've already decided. *(He takes her arm.)* And here is the house I've described to you so often!

(He tries to land a kiss, but IRINA pulls away.)

IRINA. With its awful curtains.

NIKOLAI. Irina, darling. It's a house filled with tradition!

IRINA. A tradition of tasteless furnishings.

NIKOLAI. Here I shall learn to farm as my ancestors did. Here we shall live on honest toil, eat from our own fields, make merry with the local inhabitants at harvest time.

IRINA. If I don't perish of boredom first. How far is it to the nearest ballet?

NIKOLAI. Hmmm. I'm not certain, exactly. Probably only a moderate distance. Perhaps six hundred and fifty versts.

IRINA. And just how far is a verst, anyway? I'm always forgetting.

NIKOLAI. A verst? *(He thinks.)* Isn't it three point two leagues? *(IRINA raises her arms in a how-should-I-know gesture.)* Gregor will know. And if not, here in the house you have the country branch of my family, happy to instruct you in such practical matters and to entertain you with droll family stories. They should be here shortly. Let's review. *(His delivery speeds up.)* First, there is my great-grandfather, Konstantin Alekseyevich Volnikov. My aunt, Olga Andreyevna Barkakovich, nicknamed Nika. My cousin, Pavel Sergeyevich Spivetsky, nicknamed Spavil—

(Zap sound. Blackout. Lights come up on the COMEDY. IRV is on the phone.)

IRV. I dunno, Sammy. About my age, I think. . . . Yeah, part-time as his secretary and part-time interior decorator, the last I heard. . . . Audrey. Audrey McPherson. . . . Hmmm. Let me think. . . .

(Zap sound. Blackout. Lights come up on the AVANT-GARDE PLAY. The time is the 1950s. The place is a hotel room. A MAN sits in one of the chairs, reading a brochure. A WOMAN, seen in a different posture on the couch in each scene, reclines there, staring at a crossword puzzle. Both wear white terry-cloth robes. On the floor in front of the couch, face-down, lies a dummy of a dead man, dressed in a dark business suit. The actors speak with robotic dispassion, their lines separated by longer-than-usual silences. There is a long silence before the MAN speaks.)

MAN. Apparently, this hotel is quite well appointed.

WOMAN. I need a three-letter word for "despair."

MAN. There's parking across the street for motoring guests. And all rooms are equipped with radios and telephones. *(Pause.)* "Artichoke." *(The WOMAN smiles and writes the word in her crossword.)* There's a restaurant on the second floor. . . . A concierge can be found next to the bellman's desk. . . . The staff welcomes the chance to serve us.

WOMAN. How long have we been here now?

MAN. Hmmm. Six. Or seven. Or fourteen. Or thirty-one.

WOMAN. And yet, they've still not brought up our luggage.

MAN. No doubt they're busy with other travelers.

WOMAN. And the robes from the closet are really quite comfortable. *(Pause.)*

MAN. I've read through all the hotel information, but nowhere does it say what to do in the case of a dead body in the room.

WOMAN. *(She looks down at the corpse, then pokes him experimentally with her toe.)* He seems to have been here for quite some time. Perhaps he was left by one of the other guests. *(She returns her gaze to her crossword.)* A four-letter word for "pertaining to brass family instruments."

18

MAN. You dial three for the front desk. Four for room service. Eight for housekeeping. *(Pause.)* "Bathtub."

WOMAN. *(She smiles and writes the word in.)* But no number given for the morgue?

MAN. *(He turns the brochure over and scans it in bafflement.)* No.

(Long pause, during which nothing happens. Zap sound. Blackout. Lights come up on the ENGLISH MYSTERY, as before. Immediately, there is a peal of thunder and the lights flicker off. When they come up again a moment later CLIFFORD GRAY, thirty, is in the room, in uniform and with his right arm in a sling. His manner is troubled and distant.)

EMMALINE. Clifford! You're here! Oh, darling! *(She embraces him, then gently touches his right arm.)* But what happened?

CLIFFORD. We had a visit in my trench—from one of the Kaiser's shells. Hello, Colonel, Marjorie, Reverend, Lady . . . *(He stares at LADY DENSLOW but can't think of her name.)*

LADY DENSLOW. Denslow. Vanessa. How could you forget?

CLIFFORD. *(Slightly dazed.)* Vanessa—of course. *(To the others.)* Don't let me interrupt.

19

EMMALINE. Interrupt? But, darling—you're the guest of honor.

CLIFFORD. Am I? I do pity you all. *(To INSPECTOR SWIFT.)* I don't believe we've met.

INSPECTOR SWIFT. Actually, we have. Roderick Swift. We dined together last May, in Cambridge.

EMMALINE. You remember, darling. The celebrated detective.

COL. HARDWICKE. The most famous in all England.

CLIFFORD. Memory hasn't been the same since that German shell. Sorry.

EMMALINE. You must be famished. Come, let's go into the dining room. *(CLIFFORD heads in one direction; all the rest exit in the opposite direction, except for EMMALINE, who spots CLIFFORD's mistake and rescues him.)* Oh, Clifford. This way. Don't you remember?

(Sobbing, she leads CLIFFORD off. Zap sound. Blackout. Lights come up on the SOUTHERN PLAY. The place is an antebellum mansion in Mississippi, home to the Puckett family. The time is 1934. AARON PUCKETT, twenty-five and fiery, is in the midst of a shouting match with his

father, REGINALD, who's pouring himself a whiskey from the bottle. Actors use southern accents.)

REGINALD. And what's the disgrace in living in Catfish Crossing, Mississippi?

AARON. My God, don't you have eyes? People . . . here . . . are narrow!

REGINALD. Narrow? *(Considers.)* Miz Cornford down the road—

AARON. Narrow-minded! Backward! Intolerant! Provincial! I can't breathe here, Pappy. Don't you understand? People here can't see past their crops and account books—and neither can you. No one here has time for art, or patience for anybody who does. Not *one* of the world's great watercolorists has come from Pinkham County. *That's* why I've got to go.

(Sound of train whistle. REGINALD drains his glass with one swallow.)

REGINALD. Well, go on, then! Take your two-bit paint set and those puny little brushes and go starve up north! *(He slams his glass down.)* We aren't good enough for you, is that it? Well, let me tell you, Aaron—you're not good enough for us!

21

(CAROLINE, twenty, with bizarrely stiff hair, enters in robe and slippers and shuffles straight for the whiskey. She takes no notice of the argument.)

CAROLINE. Morning, Aaron.

REGINALD. *(To AARON.)* You're a disgrace to the Puckett family!

CAROLINE. Morning, Pappy.

(CAROLINE pours the last of the whiskey into her glass, holding the bottle upside down and pounding on it like a catsup bottle to extract the last drops. She sits. Having heard this argument many times, she mouths AARON's lines and echoes his gestures.)

AARON. And how could I bring the proud name of Puckett any lower than it already is? A chimpanzee in the family would raise us up! You've drunk and gambled away what was left of the family fortune. The Depression is wiping out the rest. Grandmammy still thinks Vicksburg is under siege. Mother hanged herself in the smokehouse, right there amongst the hams. We're lucky she wasn't served that Sunday for supper. After that, you turned to moonshining, along with my "sister" Caroline—*(Indicates CAROLINE.)*—whose father everyone knows full well wasn't you, but the Fuller Brush man on this route twenty years ago, which possibly explains her hair—but no one will actually come out and say it!

REGINALD. *(Fumes a few moments in silence, then explodes.)*
And what's the matter with all that?!

(Zap sound. Blackout. Lights come up on RICHARD III, as before.)

GLOUCESTER. And if King Edward be as true and just
As I am subtle, false, and treacherous,
This day should Clarence closely be mew'd up,
About a prophecy, which says that—

(Zap sound. Blackout. Lights come up on the RUSSIAN PLAY. GLOUCESTER remains onstage, looking daggers at the audience, and finally stalks off through the Russian cast. NIKOLAI is introducing IRINA to his family: OLGA, his sickly aunt, and PAVEL, his wolfish layabout cousin, are standing. His great-grandfather KONSTANTIN, bent-backed and with a wild beard, is crossing the room with the help of a heavy staff when the lights come up.)

NIKOLAI. My maternal great-grandfather, Konstantin Alekseyevich Volnikov.

(Never pausing in his slow, staff-pounding trip across the room, wheezing KONSTANTIN glances briefly at IRINA, ignores her outstretched hands, mutters darkly, and exits.)

NIKOLAI. In time, dear Irina, a deep understanding and affection will bloom between you two. I feel sure of it.

PAVEL. *(To IRINA.)* You mustn't take his behavior personally. The old man hates everyone—not just you.

NIKOLAI. My first cousin, Pavel Sergeyevich Spivetsky.

(PAVEL kisses IRINA's hand, maintaining possession until she finally yanks it away.)

IRINA. What could have brought about such an attitude in him?

PAVEL. He thinks man is despicable and should therefore never have been created. And perhaps he has a point. *(He grins mischievously at IRINA.)*

IRINA. But then he himself would not have been born.

PAVEL. Precisely. Which is why he's been trying to kill himself for the past half century. And God, in his spite, won't let him succeed. He is now, I believe, one hundred and thirty-seven.

OLGA. Two failed poisonings. Seven botched hangings. The incident with the crossbow.

(OLGA and PAVEL share a knowing look.)

NIKOLAI. My paternal aunt, Olga Andreyevna Barkakovich.

OLGA. *(She coughs into a handkerchief.)* Don't worry about my coughing, dear. It's just a case of—*(She coughs again into the handkerchief.)*—fatal consumption.

NIKOLAI. Though may I point out that our pure country air has held back the disease for a full four decades.

OLGA. *(To IRINA.)* Is he always so cheery?

IRINA. I'm afraid so. It is a sickness of his.

OLGA. Well, nevertheless, welcome, dear child. Though what you two can mean by moving here is more than I can fathom. Pavel stays here only to escape his gambling debts. I was disappointed in love and have vowed to live out my life in the isolation of the countryside. But you—have you any notion of the tedium, the mindless allegiance to tradition, the dust—

NIKOLAI. *(Snatching the interested IRINA away.)* Come, my precious, let me introduce you to Marfa, the cook, who saw Napoleon himself pass by when she was a child and has many droll stories to tell of those fateful—

(Zap sound. Blackout. Lights come up on the COMEDY. SAMMY is prepping a nervous IRV.)

IRV. *(He addresses an imaginary woman, holding out his hand.)* Hello, I'm Moe Silverman. Hi—Moe Silverman.

25

SAMMY. Jesus, Irv. You could give yourself any name in the world, and you pick "Moe Silverman"?

IRV. All right. Mel. Mel Silverman.

SAMMY. *(He throws up his hands.)* Never mind. But while you're picking, pick yourself a new career. You want to give her what she doesn't have, and she's already got a writer on her hands. And make it snappy—she'll be here in an hour.

IRV. I told you. I already got it figured out. *(Practicing.)* Actually, Audrey, I'm a philanthropist.

SAMMY. Wow. Living in this dump?

IRV. *(Practicing.)* Though I live modestly, I direct several charitable foundations, which calls for a good deal of travel and social—

SAMMY. No, no, no. Remember? What she *doesn't* have. Her husband's a big-shot writer. Cocktail parties, autographings, the phone's ringing off the hook. She's typing his letters and mixing his drinks and taking his messages. So you offer her just the opposite. Quiet. Serenity. Selflessness.

IRV. *(Practicing.)* Actually, Audrey, I've become quite interested lately in Buddhism.

SAMMY. Mel Silverman, Buddhist philanthropist. I don't know. I think it needs work. The point is, you're someone who has time to listen to her. To pamper her.

IRV. *(Practicing.)* There's actually nothing in Buddhism opposed to sex. Or shopping.

SAMMY. You're the kind who likes to stay in on Friday night, you know . . . listening to Mozart. Plus, what'll really hook her is that unlike her lying rat of a husband, you're honest.

IRV. *(Practicing.)* And I'm extremely honest.

SAMMY. Are you crazy? You don't tell her that! If a waiter tells you the special is fabulous, do you believe him? No! You gotta let her find that out for herself. Put your high moral character on display.

IRV. Like how?

SAMMY. By puttin' down the toilet seat, for starters. *(Checks his watch.)* Hey, I'm late. Gotta run.

IRV. Yeah, and I gotta get the mess in the kitchen cleaned up.

(Both exit. Zap sound. Blackout. Lights come up on the AVANT-GARDE PLAY. A long pause.)

WOMAN. Room service was supposed to be here six hours ago.

MAN. No doubt they're busy delivering other meals.

WOMAN. *(She looks down at the corpse.)* I wonder if perhaps he died of starvation. Read the menu again. It seems to help.

MAN. *(He opens a menu.)* "All entrées come with soup or salad and choice of baked potato or coleslaw."

WOMAN. Coleslaw is one of my favorite foods.

MAN. Actually, I don't believe coleslaw is a food. What I mean to say is that it doesn't grow out of the ground. There are no silos filled with coleslaw. Coleslaw is a dish, not a food.

WOMAN. *(She faces the MAN. Pause.)* You don't love me anymore.

MAN. *(He hides behind the menu.)* "Baked salmon, served with steamed vegetables and lemon wedge. Chicken-fried steak. Meatloaf, served with succotash. T-bone steak—"

*(Zap sound. Blackout. Lights come up on the PERFOR-
MANCE ART MONOLOGUE.)*

MARSHA. *(Referring to the couple from the AVANT-GARDE*

28

PLAY.) Those guys . . . are so . . . weird. That's what they're really like. They're married, in real life. I'm telling you, even if they paid me, I would never, ever share a hotel room with them. They're trying to have a kid and if they ever do it'll be a total alien and the birth announcement will like run in the *National Enquirer*. Fortunately for humanity, I think they're just too strange to conceive. Then again, my parents did, despite being the least physical people on the planet. I swear, not even the camera crew for *Wild Kingdom* could ever catch them kissing. Frankly, I think their birth certificates are fakes and they were both raised in petri dishes. But even weirder, how could it be that such total *Best of Barry Manilow* types—I mean, my parents actually read the articles in *TV Guide*—how could they have possibly produced me? They're such paint-by-numbers, follow-the-crowd people, and I'm such an improviser. I don't have a script for this. Or for anything else. I'm not following anybody's footsteps, especially when it comes to theater. I'm going where nobody's been. Not like some of the fogies here. The ones whose watches all stopped back in the fifteen hundreds, who want to do Shakespeare over and over and over and over. And not like the ones who just like to play dress up. Like— *(Russian accent.)*—darling Irina. I mean, if you subtract out the lifts in her shoes, the tucks, the lip surgery, the wig, and the magic of silicone, the woman would totally disappear. A carcass. Even her butt's fake. One side, anyway. I forget which one. Car accident. A pin in her hip and an artificial buttock. I know, I shouldn't tell you all this, but I'm a truth-teller. It's my calling. And do I spare myself? No way! Did I come out here and pretend to feel great, the show must go on, Ethel Merman to the max? No—I told you the truth. I feel crappy! *(She opens her mouth wide toward the audience on the left, sticking out her tongue as for a doctor.)* You see all that white gunk on my throat? That's the truth. Could you see over there?

(She turns her head toward the right and opens her mouth again. Zap sound. Blackout. Lights come up on the RUSS-IAN PLAY. IRINA and NIKOLAI are looking out a window.)

NIKOLAI. —none of the ridiculous affectation of French manners here that has so infected St. Petersburg. No "Monsieur" and "Madame" and "très amusante." And no overrefined French cooking, too insubstantial for our Russian climate. Marfa, a true patriot in the kitchen, will keep us well fed on borscht and potato bread. Dear Irina, we're going to be so very happy here!

(He embraces IRINA, her back to the audience. We see one of NIKOLAI's hands creep slowly and curiously from her neck to the middle of her back, obviously heading curiously toward her fake buttock. IRINA grabs his hand from behind and breaks from his embrace. Shocked at his behavior, she peers at him with hatred.)

IRINA. But I *loathe* you! *(She realizes she's accidentally spoken her mind rather than her line.)*—I mean, borscht! And that cook of yours appears not to have washed her hands in a month.

NIKOLAI. Obsessive hand-washing, dear heart, is another French affectation. The traces of Russian soil under her nails actually help to impart a marvelous flavoring to her cuisine.

IRINA. But I take lumps of sugar, not clods of earth, in my tea.

NIKOLAI. *(Pointing out window.)* Look! There's Great-Grandfather. He really is quite charming, Irina. And he's steeped in generations of knowledge about farming. Let us take advantage of this opportunity to absorb the rural wisdom gained from his own father and grandfather and great-grandfather and great-great—

(Zap sound. Blackout. Lights come up on the ENGLISH MYSTERY. CLIFFORD, COL. HARDWICKE, and REV. SMYTHE are standing and chatting.)

COL. HARDWICKE. First-rate dinner. Can't beat English peas.

REV. SMYTHE. Though where one could find English peas in December is a mystery worthy of Inspector Swift himself.

(Clap of thunder. BEETON enters.)

CLIFFORD. Cigars, Beeton. And brandy. Bring us the best the house has to offer.

BEETON. Very good, sir. *(Exits.)*

COL. HARDWICKE. This should be something well worth sipping.

CLIFFORD. And why not? "Let us eat and drink, for tomorrow we shall die."

REV. SMYTHE. *(Looking out window.)* Still coming down hard.

CLIFFORD. How many days has it been raining here?

REV. SMYTHE. Three, isn't it?

COL. HARDWICKE. Four, actually.

CLIFFORD. Hmmm. Thirty-six to go.

REV. SMYTHE. *(Pause.)* Are you suggesting—the forty days and nights?

CLIFFORD. The timing is apt. Let's be honest, Reverend. Our species has made an absolute mess of things. Why not wipe us all out and start over?

COL. HARDWICKE. Clifford, really.

REV. SMYTHE. But God loves his children.

CLIFFORD. He's got a bloody strange way of showing it. Letting us gas and bayonet and bombard each other, living in mud and filth, smelling the rotting bodies that can't be retrieved for fear of machine-gun fire. *(To COL. HARD-WICKE.)* This isn't potting natives in India, Colonel. Not one of you has been to the front! Nor Inspector Swift either, with his putrid optimism. *(BEETON enters empty-handed, looking shaken.)* Where *is* Swift, come to think of it? And Beeton, where are the bloody brandy and cigars?

BEETON. Please forgive me, sir. But Inspector Swift— Inspector Swift, sir, is dead.

(Clap of thunder. CLIFFORD cowers at the sound.)

COL. HARDWICKE. Dead? Is this some sort of joke?

REV. SMYTHE. Lord protect us.

CLIFFORD. *(To BEETON.)* Speak, man.

BEETON. After dining, he used the telephone in the study, sir, to make an urgent call, so he said. When I knocked, so as to fetch the cigars, there was no answer. I knocked again, then finally looked in. And there he was, slumped on the floor. When I checked his pulse . . . *(He trails off.)*

COL. HARDWICKE. Our foremost detective—himself the victim of murder.

REV. SMYTHE. Murder? We have no knowledge that it was murder.

(All turn in unison to face COL. HARDWICKE.)

COL. HARDWICKE. Quite right. Dashed hasty of me. Been reading too many mystery novels of late. *(He forces a laugh.)* Let's have a look at the body. My wife was a nurse. Perhaps there's still hope.

(ALL exit. Zap sound. Blackout. Lights come up on RICHARD III, act 1, midway in scene 2. GLOUCESTER and LADY ANNE face each other across the corpse of King Henry VI—the same male corpse from the AVANT-GARDE PLAY but now with a crown on its head and lying on the couch. GLOUCESTER wears a dagger-bearing scabbard.)

GLOUCESTER. I did not kill your husband.

LADY ANNE. Why, then he is alive.

GLOUCESTER. Nay, he is dead; and slain by—

(The phone rings. GLOUCESTER whirls and glares into the wings. It rings again. He whips out his dagger and brings it down onto the telephone table, severing the cord. He lifts up the phone, crosses the room, triumphantly drops it into the wastebasket, and returns.)

GLOUCESTER. He is dead; and slain by Edward's hand.

LADY ANNE. In thy foul throat thou liest: Queen Margaret saw
Thy murderous falchion smoking in his blood;
The which thou once didst bend against her breast,
But that thy brothers—

(Zap sound. Lights out briefly, then back on. MAN and WOMAN from the AVANT-GARDE PLAY have partially made their entrance. The Shakespeareans are still in place. LADY ANNE looks in dismay at GLOUCESTER, then both stare accusingly at the audience. GLOUCESTER sighs, snatches the crown off the corpse's head, and disgustedly rolls the corpse from the couch to the floor with a thud as he and LADY ANNE exit. MAN and WOMAN take their places. WOMAN erases a word in her crossword puzzle. MAN reads a newspaper. After a time, he turns the page. WOMAN gently clears her throat, but no words follow. Zap sound. Blackout. Lights come up on the SOUTHERN PLAY, as before.)

AARON. *(Continuing his litany of complaints.)* Aunt

Cordelia's in the asylum in Tupelo, hoarding the sugar cubes from the dining room and giving 'em to all the young doctors she tries to seduce.

(Sound of train whistle. CAROLINE drains the last sip of whiskey from her glass and regards it.)

CAROLINE. Mighty fine breakfast. What's for dinner?

AARON. Everyone's waiting for Grandmammy to die, to hear the twenty-seventh revision to her will—

CAROLINE. Lawyer was here again yesterday.

REGINALD. Twenty-eighth.

AARON. Everyone cozying up to her in the most repulsive fashion, in hopes of getting River Oaks, her twenty-thousand-acre estate—

(LUKE enters. He's thirty and wildly energetic, caroming around the room, picking up and putting down objects, chuckling to himself—the very opposite of the character Aaron describes. All stare at him in bafflement.)

AARON. While everyone knows that my stepbrother Luke, here—who's hardly left his room for years, just hunched up in the closet, in the dark, hardly speaking—

LUKE. *(Hearty and loud.)* Howdy, all!

AARON. *(Pointedly to actor playing Luke.)* And *hardly moving,* just like the salamanders he raises in his closet. Which is all he's done since the fateful day he came upon Grandpappy's body down by the river—

CAROLINE. *(To REGINALD.)* This boy do go on, don't he.

(Zap sound. Blackout. Lights come up on the PERFORMANCE ART MONOLOGUE.)

MARSHA. So like my father is the manager of Planet Snooze, this store that's as big as a freaking galaxy that just sells beds. His one goal in the universe is to put people to sleep. Yawning was considered a big conversation starter in my house. "You going to sleep soon?" "Did you get a nap in today?" And then in the morning, every morning—the sleep report. "So how did you sleep?" "OK, I guess." "Just OK? Let's talk about that later. How 'bout you, Mother?" "Oh, my, I had a wonderful sleep." *(She sniffles loudly.)* God, I've got to take something for this cold. Hold on. *(She fishes a pill out of a pocket, looks in vain for something to wash it down with, discovers that the whiskey bottle is empty, and throws up her hands.)* Oh, well. There's always saliva. *(She stops talking, spends five seconds collecting saliva in her mouth, then manages to squeeze the pill down her throat.)* My mother stayed home till I was in middle school. Then she got a part-time job out at the mall at Jingle Bell Lane, one of those shops that sells Christmas crap the whole freaking year. The place is like on permanent pause. It's always December there. There's always fake snow on the windowpanes. Maybe you'd stop aging if you like barricaded yourself inside and never left. If you could stand "The Twelve Days of Christmas" playing nonstop. You want to set me off, start singing that song. And that stupid fake scent in those shops. Christmas is supposed to smell good by itself, without Dow Chemical. I swear that stuff affected my mother's brain. She's got this sort of bulgy forehead, probably because the part of the brain devoted to gift selection and home decoration is like totally huge and has swallowed up the parts for fashion and musical taste. Both my parents worked in these weird island worlds—no racism, sexism, pollution, assassinations, riots. Like they never happened. I swear, if you went into Planet Snooze and screamed "Martin Luther King!" in my father's face, he'd say, "You bet. We've got loads of kings." Can you imagine being an only child, marooned with these loonies? Where was Child Protective Services? It was like living in a freaking morgue. I should have gotten free antidepressants in my school lunch. Not too much, like that new guy playing Luke—*(Gestures toward the wings.)*—who I think maybe got his diet pill uppers mixed up with his Tic Tacs and took like a few dozen too many. So anyway, growing up with—

(Zap sound. Blackout. Lights come up on the SOUTHERN PLAY, as before. Luke is still bouncing around the room.)

AARON. And personally, I've always felt that Luke's salamanders were metaphors for his desire to burrow into the darkness, to escape the horrible memory of—

(Luke is too wired to remember his southern accent or even that he's in a play.)

LUKE. What horrible memory?

(REGINALD, CAROLINE, and AARON exchange worried looks.)

CAROLINE. *(Improvising.)* My, what a northern southern accent you've got, Luke. Calm yourself. And tell us about Belle.

LUKE. Belle?

REGINALD AND AARON. *(Shouting.)* Belle!

(This jars LUKE's memory.)

LUKE. Oh, yeah. *(Puts on southern accent and rushes madly through his lines.)* I think Belle might be hurt. She's my favorite salamander. She's the one I found down by the river. You know the place. You all do. Down there where they found the—found the—found the body, found Grandpappy's body. *(Having finished his speech, he resumes moving around the stage, stops next to CAROLINE, and speaks without an accent.)* So what are you doing after the show?

*(Zap sound. Blackout. Lights come up on the COMEDY. A
Mozart slow movement is playing. IRV is finishing showing AUDREY McPHERSON, a harried forty-year-old,
around the apartment. She finds herself eyeing the books in
the bookcase.)*

AUDREY. Lot of books.

IRV. Yeah. I—I like reading. You know.

AUDREY. Irving Weinstein, I see. A whole shelf of 'em. You
a fan?

IRV. *(Flustered.)* Yeah. Sort of. He's, you know, pretty
good. Underrated, actually.

AUDREY. He's a friend of my husband's.

IRV. No kidding. Wow. Wonder what he's like.

AUDREY. *(Absently, while scanning books.)* A heaping plate
of neuroses, I hear.

IRV. You don't say. *(Chews on this bitterly.)* I wouldn't have
guessed that. *(Tries to put it behind him, gestures toward the
room.)* So what do you think? Speaking as a professional
decorator.

AUDREY. Well, it's certainly got potential. I like your idea of increasing the sense of sanctuary, of making it a place of peace and meditation. Couldn't we all use that. You'd have to be flexible, of course. The couch, for instance.

IRV. I think I could be very flexible on the couch. *(Roguish smile.)* Then again, it was my grandmother's. Loyalty means a lot to me. Loyalty and fidelity. Fidelity and honesty.

AUDREY. That's refreshing. And clients' sentiments certainly have to be taken into account. *(She sits down on the couch.)*

IRV. They certainly do. Say. It's after five. You must be done for today. Can I get you a drink?

AUDREY. You must have read my mind. I'd love one.

IRV. Comin' up.

AUDREY. It's been an absolutely crazy week. I swear this is the first time I've sat down in days. *(AUDREY settles into the couch and closes her eyes. IRV walks suavely toward the whiskey, holds up the empty bottle, gestures toward the wings, engages in a long, mimed conversation unseen by AUDREY, and eventually dips two glasses into the nearby fishbowl. Meanwhile:)* You like Mozart, Mr. Silverman?

IRV. Moe.

AUDREY. Moe.

IRV. I mean Mel!

AUDREY. Mel.

IRV. Moe's my middle name.

AUDREY. *(To herself.)* Mel Moe Silverman.

IRV. Yeah, Mozart's probably my favorite. . . . Right up there with . . . with . . . you know, the other great . . . music writers.

(He brings the glasses, discreetly shaking his head at AUDREY, trying to tell her not to drink.)

AUDREY. God, you're a savior. Thank you. *(She beams, takes no notice of IRV's hint, clinks glasses with him, and takes a gulp. She smiles.)* I used to—(*The taste hits her. She grimaces and gives a mighty shudder, registers IRV's headshaking, and peers at her glass. Her mind is on what she's swallowed, not her lines, which she delivers flatly.)*—play Mozart on the piano. But that was a long time ago. *(She wipes her mouth on her sleeve.)* My husband only likes jazz, which after a while makes me want to run out of the apartment.

IRV. You can always come here. It's always calm and—*(Polka music comes up from below.)* Calm and tranquil. *(IRV*

42

taps his toe on the floor, to no effect.) Tranquil and appealing. *(He pounds louder.)* Appealing and— *(He jumps up and down on floor several times. The polka music stops.)*—and calm.

AUDREY. This drink's going to my head.

IRV. You need something in your stomach. Feel like eating?

AUDREY. *(Forgetting her character, thinking of her stomach.)* No! *(Remembering her character, but with no enthusiasm in her voice.)* I mean, yes. I'd love to.

IRV. Right around the corner there's this great little— *(Reluctantly.)* seafood place—

(AUDREY stiffens. She sniffs her drink. Her eyes cut to the fishbowl, then to IRV. She speaks her next line as if ready to murder him.)

AUDREY. How did you know? I adore seafood.

IRV. *(Fearfully.)* Great. Let's go.

(They stand. Zap sound. Blackout. Lights come up on the RUSSIAN PLAY. KONSTANTIN is holding forth to a seated IRINA and NIKOLAI, his delivery maddeningly slow. He holds his staff in one hand.)

KONSTANTIN. —nothing more important, you see, in the

43

cultivation of beets, than the soil. Nothing. The condition of the soil is paramount. This cannot be stressed too highly. As my great-grandfather was fond of saying, an aphorism for which he was known far and wide, for dozens of versts in every direction, as he was wont to say—indeed he said it nearly every day, sometimes, actually, more often—as he liked to say, "Good soil—good beets."

(KONSTANTIN smiles, awaiting response. IRINA stifles a yawn. NIKOLAI produces a pen and tiny notebook.)

NIKOLAI. Let me write that down.

KONSTANTIN. *(Repeating words slowly for NIKOLAI's benefit.)* Good . . . soil . . . good—

(Zap sound. Blackout. Lights come up on the ENGLISH MYSTERY. CLIFFORD, COL. and MRS. HARDWICKE, REV. SMYTHE, LADY DENSLOW, and EMMALINE are all standing.)

COL. HARDWICKE. —propose that we all recount to the group as a whole all our movements, from the time dinner finished to the present, leaving out no detail, however seemingly unimportant.

EMMALINE. Good thinking.

MRS. HARDWICKE. No detail *whatsoever.*

COL. HARDWICKE. Marjorie, why don't you begin.

MRS. HARDWICKE. Very well. Let me see. After the dessert, which I thought was quite lovely—I've always been quite partial to custard—Lady Denslow and I began chatting, didn't we, first off, about her dress, which I could never wear, not with that neckline, but which on her really does look—

(Zap sound. Blackout. Lights come up on the AVANT-GARDE PLAY. MAN is holding a street map in front of his face. He unfolds it dramatically. WOMAN is miming knitting with pleasant concentration, using neither yarn nor needles. He notices her.)

MAN. Do you enjoy knitting?

WOMAN. Oh, yes. Very much.

MAN. And yet I notice you don't use yarn or needles.

WOMAN. That's the way my mother taught me. And what with the price of yarn these days . . .

(MAN mutters in agreement, then turns his map to study a different portion. Silence. Zap sound. Blackout. Lights come up on the SOUTHERN PLAY. GRANDMAMMY, ancient and wearing a white dress, is sitting in a chair. She holds a glass of iced tea. Facing her is LUKE, fidgeting

madly, scarcely able to stay put on the couch. He uses his southern accent in this scene.)

GRANDMAMMY. You've always been my favorite, Luke.

LUKE. Why's that, Grandmammy?

GRANDMAMMY. Reckon it goes back, way back to when I was just a knee-baby. Back before the Yankees set their guns on Vicksburg.

LUKE. You know I love your stories, Grandmammy.

GRANDMAMMY. And it's a long story I'm fixing to tell. *(Clearly addressing the actor playing LUKE.)* So get comfortable!

(She takes a deep breath preparatory to beginning her tale. Zap sound. Blackout. Lights come up on the RUSSIAN PLAY, as before. IRINA has slumped down farther in her seat.)

KONSTANTIN. A salty soil is good for beets. How do you tell, you ask? Well, I'll tell you. What you do is this. First, you take a little pinch in your hand. Not a great deal. Just a pinch. Then you put a bit of that on your tongue—

(Zap sound. Blackout. Lights come up on the ENGLISH MYSTERY, as before.)

MRS. HARDWICKE. —and I told her I thought the sleeves were darling, and then we spoke of the war, and when it might end, and what we would wear when it did—

(Zap sound. Blackout. Lights come up on the SOUTHERN PLAY, as before.)

GRANDMAMMY. —but General Grant didn't count on Vicksburg holding out this long. No sir, he—*(The phone rings.)* That must be the lawyer. Got a change I want to make. *(Phone continues ringing. She addresses actor playing Luke.)* Aren't you gonna *answer* it?

(LUKE bustles to the phone table, finds the phone gone, looks into wings, then searches the room for it, while the phone continues ringing. He's forgotten his southern accent.)

LUKE. We never had this problem before.

GRANDMAMMY. Well, we never shared a house with no uppity royal family before. Look in the wastebasket!

(Luke crouches by wastebasket, picks up the receiver, and puts it to his ear. Ringing stops.)

LUKE. Hello. *(He listens. To GRANDMAMMY.)* Nobody there.

GRANDMAMMY. *(Rolls her eyes, then addresses audience.)* Y'all go on to another play. I need to talk to this boy a minute.

(Zap sound. Blackout. Lights come up on the RUSSIAN PLAY, as before. IRINA is now asleep.)

KONSTANTIN. Of course, if you should see black spots on the leaves, that tells you something. Something important! *(He pounds his staff on the floor for emphasis, waking up IRINA.)* I cannot emphasize that enough.

NIKOLAI. *(Writing in notebook.)* Black . . .

KONSTANTIN. *(Repeating for NIKOLAI.)* Black . . .

(Zap sound. Blackout. Lights come up on the ENGLISH MYS-TERY, as before.)

MRS. HARDWICKE. —how lovely it would be if the war were to end in the springtime, because I have this absolutely precious linen dress with a brocade bodice—

(Zap sound. Blackout. Lights come up on the PERFOR-MANCE ART MONOLOGUE.)

MARSHA. Wow. You natives are restless tonight. *(Sneezes. She takes the bandanna off her head, blows her nose into it, can't decide what to do with it, and puts it back on her head.)*

So anyway, my family lived in the suburbs, naturally. And my parents, naturally, picked the newest, stupidest suburb to live in. And, naturally, our street had a stupid name. So stupid, I'm too embarrassed to say it. *(Silently debates whether to tell.)* All right, all right. Gotta tell the freaking truth. Burbling Rivulet Court. These developers like suddenly turn into American Indians when they name their streets. Probably his son was named Pees on Toilet Seat. My father actually liked the name. Naturally. And my mother appreciated the shag carpeting in the bathrooms and the sparkly finish on the walls. I was twelve when we moved there from the city and I thought it sucked. The whole neighborhood looked fake, like it had been built by some model train nut. I kept expecting to see this giant hand reach down. Maybe, I thought, we were only an inch high and we were actually living in some weirdo's basement. That would have at least been more exciting. There were all kinds of lawsuits against the developer for sewer problems, heating problems, mold problems, karma problems, so practically half the houses were empty. After living downtown, it was like being shipwrecked. The closest store was like two miles away at a mall. No wonder I got into make-believe. It was the only way to escape from Burbling freaking Rivulet Court. First, I started calling myself Alexandra instead of Marsha. Then I switched from Alexandra to Atlantis. My parents totally refused to go along and change my name on all the legal papers and stuff, so I finally had to go back to Marsha, kind of like—*(English accent.)* "Clifford," with his arm in the sling, who was born a woman, then he went through all the treatments and operations and became a guy and married that dolt who plays Lady Denslow, but then, I don't know, maybe it was the hair on his back or having to wear boring men's clothes, but he told me, like in private, that he's started cross-dressing and is kinda thinking about *going back* to being a woman—especially with the big lingerie sale at Macy's—

(Zap sound. Blackout. Lights come up on the ENGLISH MYSTERY. CLIFFORD and EMMALINE are alone in the room.)

EMMALINE. Oh, Clifford—I'm so frightened!

(She runs toward him, then seems to recall MARSHA's revelation and pulls up short of the expected embrace. The following exchange is delivered with trepidation by the actors, the words reverberating with coincidental double meaning.)

CLIFFORD. Don't be afraid, Emmaline. I'm here.

EMMALINE. But you haven't—you haven't seemed like yourself.

CLIFFORD. No one comes back from there unchanged.

EMMALINE. But I never expected—this.

CLIFFORD. I know it must be a shock to you.

EMMALINE. I feel I hardly know you.

(LADY DENSLOW saunters onstage, glaring at CLIFFORD. She speaks without a British accent.)

LADY DENSLOW. Yeah. Me, too.

EMMALINE. I'm sure everything must be quite disorienting for you.

CLIFFORD. You've no idea. *(Dropping character, fingering his uniform's buttons.)* I'd just gotten used to having buttons on the right.

(Zap sound. Blackout. Lights come up on the PERFORMANCE ART MONOLOGUE.)

MARSHA. I wanted to act. Not that anyone in my town knew anything about any form of culture whatsoever, except what they'd picked up on *Jeopardy!* I mean, let's face the truth. Living in the suburbs is about shopping. Pure and simple. Every person, get it, is like King Tut. And every person's house is like King Tut's freaking tomb. The more crammed with crap, the better. *(Imitating wife, then husband.)* "Look at this darling set of ceramic finger bowls I picked up on sale." "That's wonderful dear, even though we've never unwrapped the ones we have." "Well, of course, I expect to do quite a bit more entertaining in the afterlife." Instead of the Egyptian

Book of the Dead, people have the Williams-Sonoma catalog. And since you can't buy art and literature at the mall, it must not be worth anything, right? There's some chemical they put in the water in the suburbs that keeps people from seeing how totally clueless they are. Except for me. I drank bottled water. So I got into drama, except in middle school the only play we put on was *Annie,* which the whole eighth grade class did. I tried out for the lead. Mrs. Hoffmeister gave it to Sylvia Scapellini and put me on stage crew because she hated my guts because I did some research and found out she *hadn't* been married to Harrison Ford after all—

(Zap sound. Blackout. Lights come up on RICHARD III, act 3, scene 1. PRINCE EDWARD, wearing a crown, enters to sound of trumpet flourish. GLOUCESTER and BUCKINGHAM enter from the other direction.)

BUCKINGHAM. Welcome, sweet prince, to London,
    to your chamber.

GLOUCESTER. Welcome, dear cousin, my thoughts'
    sovereign;
The weary way hath made you melancholy.

PRINCE. No, uncle, but our crosses on the way
Have made it tedious, wearisome—*(Zap sound. Blackout, but only for an instant as the furious GLOUCESTER stamps his foot, causing the lights to come back up.)*—and heavy:
I want more uncles here to welcome me.

GLOUCESTER. Sweet prince, the untainted virtue of
    your years—*(The zap sound is repeated. No blackout.
    GLOUCESTER again raises his hand in a "Stop"
    gesture toward the wings while facing the PRINCE and
    continuing his lines.)*
Hath not yet div'd into the world's deceit—

*(GLOUCESTER emphasizes those last three words, turning
    his gaze on the audience. The zap sound is heard three
    times in a row. Blackout. After a longer than normal
    period of darkness and sounds of a scuffle, lights come up
    on the RUSSIAN PLAY. IRINA and PAVEL are stand-
    ing alone. We hear a mournful tune played on a bal-
    alaika.)*

IRINA. *(Cocking ear to the music.)* What is that dreadful,
depressing music?

PAVEL. Your husband asked a few peasants to play him some
of their traditional tunes.

IRINA. But that's been going on for hours now! The lazy
rascals are supposed to be working in the fields!

PAVEL. Your husband is blissfully blind to human evil, from
the laziness of the peasants to the thieving of the servants to
my own much more grievous sins. Though what we all find
even more remarkable about him is that he actually appears
to like the provinces. Never in life or in literature have I

encountered such a man. The dearth of stimulation, the contempt for the arts, the coarse food—

IRINA. I believe I would kill to get my hands on a croissant right now.

PAVEL. It quite baffles me. Frankly, Irina, I wonder how a woman of your refinement will bear it.

IRINA. I swear, I would murder a harmless old woman for one of those Parisian raspberry tarts—

PAVEL. It will be very difficult.

IRINA. —with that delicate, buttery crust—

PAVEL. Very difficult, indeed. Unless, of course, you find comfort . . . elsewhere.

(PAVEL has been slowly approaching IRINA. He now takes her in his arms. They embrace passionately. After several seconds, the audience sees one of his hands moving in the air, trying to decide which buttock to sample. IRINA senses this and grabs his hand just in time. She pulls quickly away and must force her next line out of her mouth.)

IRINA. Oh, Pavel, the touch of your fingers so—*(With the greatest reluctance.)*—thrills me. Without you—

(Zap sound. Blackout. Lights come up on the COMEDY. IRV is parading around the room, holding a strip of photos and triumphantly reporting to SAMMY.)

IRV. You wouldn't have believed it.

SAMMY. Yeah?

IRV. I'm telling you, she was eating out of my hand!

SAMMY. I just hope you washed your hand first, better than your dishes.

IRV. So we have this long, quiet dinner together. Max had just left town for an autographing. She has a glass of wine, then another, then a third, and pretty soon she's telling me what a jerk he is. Other women on the side, screams orders at her, blows up if she spends a dime on herself.

SAMMY. Not like our philanthropist here. How'd you pay for the meal?

IRV. Got a credit card offer in the mail that morning.

SAMMY. So then what?

IRV. So then, we go out strolling. It had cooled off. It was gorgeous out. I take her for ice cream and tell her all about Marie.

SAMMY. Marie who?

IRV. Marie, my wife who died donating a kidney for a distant relative.

SAMMY. *(Affected.)* No kidding.

IRV. Of course I'm kidding! I made her up. She's Mel's wife. To stimulate sympathy.

SAMMY. Man, you fiction writers are brutal.

IRV. So we're walking around, and we pass one of those booths that takes your picture. She's still kind of tipsy and giggly. We go in. We have a ball. And every time the flash goes off, instead of "cheese," I'm thinking, "Hi, Max."

(IRV gives the strip of photos to SAMMY.)

SAMMY. Wow. She's kissing your cheek in the last one.

IRV. The camera never lies.

SAMMY. So then?

IRV. So then, I walk her over to her place on the East Side.

SAMMY. One of the more inexpensive modes of travel. And then?

IRV. And then, we kiss on the doorstep.

SAMMY. You packed your 3-in-One oil? *(IRV snatches photo strip from SAMMY.)* And then?

IRV. And then I walked home.

SAMMY. You walked home? For a writer, you're not much on love scenes.

IRV. Hey—I don't have to be. Mission accomplished. When Max sees these, he'll write the scene for me. He gets back the day after tomorrow. I'm gonna knock on his door and give 'em to him. And, man, when I do, all the money he's making off my life suddenly ain't gonna—

(A clap of thunder. IRV and SAMMY look confused.)

SAMMY. *(Obviously improvising.)* Guess a little storm . . . must have blown in. *(Another clap of thunder. IRV taps his foot on the floor experimentally. Another thunderclap. IRV pounds harder.)* I just hope your neighbor, the one with the *polka records,* remembered to close his windows. *(IRV and SAMMY wait expectantly for polka music. Long pause. Trumpet flourish from the last RICHARD III segment. IRV and SAMMY look at each other.)* You expecting somebody . . . important?

(Zap sound. Blackout. Lights come up on the AVANT-GARDE PLAY. The MAN has his ear to one of the walls. The WOMAN is knitting.)

MAN. I'm sure of it. A man. And a woman. The man is giving a tip to the bellboy.

WOMAN. What do they look like?

MAN. *(Concentrates awhile.)* I can't tell.

WOMAN. I wonder if there's a corpse in their room, too.

MAN. They haven't mentioned one.

WOMAN. Do you suppose they'll charge us for our corpse, even though we didn't order it?

MAN. It's best not to get into arguments with the staff. That was mentioned several times in the hotel information. *(A pause.)* She's commenting on the lovely view. They look out on the lake.

WOMAN. *(Speaking with emotion for the first time.)* But there is no lake here. Not in any direction.

MAN. The man is eating the mints off the pillow.

WOMAN. We never had any mints on ours.

MAN. He says they're quite good.

WOMAN. But it's not bedtime yet! Pound on the wall! Make him stop!

MAN. Apparently, they've brought their Chihuahua.

WOMAN. But you read that pets weren't allowed! The hotel brochure specifically mentioned that!

MAN. The dog's name is Gringo.

WOMAN. That's not fair! We were going to name our Chihuahua Gringo, if we ever got one. They get to have everything!

(A woman's scream is heard through the wall.)

MAN. Wait. *(Pause.)* They have a corpse.

WOMAN. *(Composed again.)* Well. That's a relief.

(Zap sound. Blackout. Lights come up on the SOUTHERN PLAY. A dummy of a female corpse, wearing a white dress like GRANDMAMMY's and clearly distinguishable from the male corpse in black, lies face-down on the floor in front of the chair GRANDMAMMY last occupied. REGINALD and CAROLINE are gathered around, while LUKE bounces around the room. He uses a southern accent.)

LUKE. —all scrambled up about her great-great-grandfather's family comin' over in 1780 and how they left England so they'd be free to cook their meat according to how the Bible teaches, which is barbecue, and how iced tea's mentioned in Scripture, too, only by a different name, and when I come back from getting her more tea in the kitchen, there she was, dead on the floor.

REGINALD. *(He stares down at the corpse.)* Grandmammy!

CAROLINE. *(Heads toward whiskey bottle.)* Lord! I need a—*(She picks up the empty bottle, looks toward the wings, then improvises.)*—a chance to . . . reflect on . . . the subject of . . . this startling development.

REGINALD. *(Stares suspiciously at LUKE.)* And you two were alone?

LUKE. Yup. Just us.

REGINALD. *(Looks around.)* Where's Aaron?

CAROLINE. Didn't you know? Packed his paints and walked to the station. Moving to New York City.

LUKE. *(To CAROLINE, without accent.)* You want to go to my place after we're done?

(CAROLINE ignores LUKE, who moves around the room,

observing the scene from various angles like an interested spectator.)

REGINALD. Wonder what she died of.

CAROLINE. Maybe one of them Yankee shells hung up in the air for seventy-five years and finally hit her on the head.

REGINALD. That, or one of her own relations. Someone who'd had a look at her will—and didn't want no more changes bein' made.

(A pause. REGINALD and CAROLINE exchange glances. AARON walks in, carrying a suitcase, and approaches the corpse. REGINALD directs his words to him.)

REGINALD. Someone who'd have an alibi tighter than a preacher's collar. *(Pause.)* Thought you were on your way to New York City.

AARON. Missed the train. What happened to Grandmammy? Is she—is she dead?

REGINALD. As dead as you are dumb, boy. How many times have you missed that train goin' north?

AARON. Hmmm. Well, once—today.

REGINALD. And?

AARON. Twice yesterday.

REGINALD. And?

AARON. Twice on Friday. Once on Thursday. Three times on Wednesday.

CAROLINE. Same as last week.

REGINALD. And every time, we gotta have the same long-winded argument before you go. It's your way of trying to kill me, ain't it? You're aimin' to drive up my blood pressure and put me in the grave!

CAROLINE. With all those trains you missed, Aaron, some people might be entertaining doubts that you're ready to leave Catfish Crossing and become one of the world's great watercolorists.

REGINALD. And others might be entertaining thoughts that with your knowledge of paints, it wouldn't be hard for you to slip something fatal into Grandmammy's iced tea.

AARON. *(He drops his suitcase with a thud and faces REGINALD.)* You would accuse your own son—of the crime of murdering your own mother?

REGINALD. *(Pause. He looks at the others for support, swelling with exasperation, then shouts:)* And what's the matter with that?!

CAROLINE. Nothing, Pappy. Calm yourself. Nothing at all. *(She looks up.)* And nothing at all is what we might be getting in the will. Reckon we better go find it.

(ALL scatter offstage, hopping over the corpse. Zap sound. Blackout. Lights come up on the ENGLISH MYSTERY. The dummy of the female corpse remains where it is. LADY DENSLOW and REV. SMYTHE are looking down at it. CLIFFORD enters.)

CLIFFORD. Good God—not Mrs. Hardwicke!

REV. SMYTHE. It happened when the storm knocked out the lights.

LADY DENSLOW. Strangled.

REV. SMYTHE. There can be no doubt now that there's a murderer among us.

LADY DENSLOW. *(Heavily, to CLIFFORD.)* Someone whose surface appearance is a sham.

CLIFFORD. Don't be daft. I could hardly have strangled her with this arm of mine.

LADY DENSLOW. *(Bitterly, she abandons the script along with her English accent for the rest of the scene.)* Then perhaps you took off one of *my* high heels and bludgeoned her to death with it.

(CLIFFORD and REV. SMYTHE look at each other, unsure what to do. REV. SMYTHE tries to return to the script.)

REV. SMYTHE. We must take stock of the situation, and quickly. What do we know?

LADY DENSLOW. *(To CLIFFORD.)* We know how the seams in my blouses got ripped.

CLIFFORD. *(Abandoning the script.)* Judy—

REV. SMYTHE. *(Improvising, trying to make peace.)* The Bible, of course, teaches compassion, for all our—all our—

LADY DENSLOW. The Bible, if I'm not mistaken, calls for stoning in this case.

REV. SMYTHE. Lady Denslow—

LADY DENSLOW. Not that you, *Reverend,* should be casting stones at anyone.

REV. SMYTHE. Judy—

LADY DENSLOW. Not with two convictions for wifebeating. I saw Margo at the bus stop in front of the hospital this morning. Or I think it was her—hard to tell with the dark glasses and hat. What does Jesus recommend for such a nasty temper?

*(REV. SMYTHE glares at LADY DENSLOW. Breathing heav-
ily, building up to an explosion, he returns to the script but
in the voice of a raging maniac, his wrathful face turned
toward LADY DENSLOW.)*

REV. SMYTHE. The thunder is coming close upon the
lightning! The storm would appear to be nearly overhead! If
the lights go again, we may be . . . IN DANGER!

*(Lightning flashes. All cover their ears in preparation for
thunder. Long pause. Then we hear the polka music from
the COMEDY. Cast slowly uncovers ears in bafflement.
Zap sound. Blackout. Polka music continues to play. Lights
come up on the PERFORMANCE ART MONOLOGUE.
MARSHA rolls her eyes, waiting for the music to stop,
which it finally does.)*

MARSHA. Whoa. Polka music coming out of the sky. What
a concept. Book of Revelation, the Sequel. Actually, there's
a perfectly rational explanation. Our totally irrational sound
person—who's like ready to crack even if everything's perfect and the weather's sunny and seventy degrees and there's
no bad news anywhere in the world—he walked off the set.
Ran, actually. Too much pressure. Taught first grade at this
magnet school for hyperactive kids a few years ago. Pushed
him over the edge. He can't take too much activity. Post-
Noisy-Cafeteria Syndrome. Kind of like Mr. Mycroft, my
high-school drama teacher. Nervous like a rabbit. Afraid of
the principal. Afraid of parents, the superintendent, the

school board, his mother, the tooth fairy. So like when I lobbied for us to put on *The Crucible*—forget it. Might be offensive to pagans, or Christians, or Massachuso-Americans. The same with every other play that had any teeth at all. So what did we put on? *Arsenic and Old Lace,* that shocking exposé of the boarding-house industry that scandalized Broadway and traumatized millions—not. And then there was *Harvey,* about the guy who sees the imaginary rabbit, and *The Sound of Music,* to keep the big yodeling voting bloc happy, and *A Midsummer Night's Dream*—and absolutely nothing about what was actually happening in the world! So finally, in my senior year, I said, "Screw this." Enough with the rabbits and the mountain goats. It was time to bring on the rats and the roaches. Time to put the real world onstage. So I created my first piece, about how the world sucks and people should quit denying it and get in touch with their sadness and disappointment. It was called *Send in the Frowns.* The first performance was at lunch on the school auditorium steps, where lots of students used to eat. I memorized this spiel about something sad from my life—how on my birthdays my father never signed the card, like he wasn't actually involved in my birth, which was liberating, true, but also creepy, and how my mother every year bought me some present for someone like five years younger than I was. Then, after that, I asked people in the audience to come up and tell something sad from their lives. Which nobody would do. Great. So I winged it and told how the year I was fourteen and my parents were the most impossible they'd ever been, they left out where I'd see it this brochure for a female military school called Camp Opportunity, and how I got an article on lobotomies and left it nonchalantly taped to their bathroom mirror. So then I asked again for volunteers. Nobody. By this time, there were like four people left. So I just kept telling stuff from my life. And it hit me: I didn't need the freaking audience and their memories. I also didn't need costumes or sets or trapdoors or greasy makeup. And I didn't need scripts. No more plots about dukes and fairy queens. No memorizing and underlining. No stupid "fourth wall" between the stage and the seats. No characters. Reality! Me! I threw out the entire theater tradition—and then I climbed in the trash can and jumped on it! Instead, I told the truth. The truth that nobody'd ever told: how dead life is in the suburbs, how people there have no time for culture, how families can be totally weird, how people you trust turn out to be lying scums—*(The zap sound is heard, the stage goes dark, but MARSHA keeps talking.)* See! Exactly what I'm talking about! The truth makes you nervous, you pathetic wimps!

(The zap sound is repeated and lights come up on the RUSS-IAN PLAY. KONSTANTIN enters with his staff and begins making his painfully slow way across the stage, wheezing noisily.)

(Zap sound. Blackout. Lights come up on RICHARD III, act 4, scene 2. RICHARD enters, now wearing crown and royal robes, followed by BUCKINGHAM. RICHARD halts, grimaces, turns toward the wings, mimes playing

trumpet, and awaits the sound of a trumpet flourish. Silence. Then we hear the train whistle from the SOUTHERN PLAY. RICHARD glares at the wings; BUCKINGHAM covers his eyes.)

(Zap sound. Blackout. Lights come up on the SOUTHERN PLAY. CAROLINE, still wearing robe and slippers, enters alone and frantically searches the room for the will.)

(Zap sound. Blackout. Lights come up on the RUSSIAN PLAY, as before. KONSTANTIN is now halfway across the room.)

(Zap sound. Blackout. Lights come up on the AVANT-GARDE play. The WOMAN knits with great concentration. The MAN is hidden behind the outstretched map. He crosses his legs. He uncrosses them.)

(Zap sound. Blackout. Lights come up on the COMEDY. A speechless, panicked IRV is retreating before a love-bewitched, fast-talking AUDREY, who's blown into the apartment with a suitcase in one hand and a cat carrier in the other.)

AUDREY. —and I was walking along, seeing your face in my mind and thinking how very dear to me you'd become in such a short time, and how I didn't think I could live without that face in my life, and your gentle voice, and your kindness and generosity and your honesty. And then I got home and there was Max, telling me how you'd come over that morning to tell him about us, and I knew right then that we were perfect for each other, that our thoughts were aligned, and our values, and soon our lives. And I didn't even care when Max screamed and swore. It was you I was seeing, not him. And when he told me to pack up and leave, they were the happiest words I ever heard. I didn't bring much. Tomorrow I'll call the moving company. And with your wanting to simplify and pare down your possessions, there'll be plenty of room. And the cats are indoor, so the move won't faze them. *(Sound of cat yowling. Audrey speaks to the cat carrier in a cutesy voice.)* Yes, I know, Mommy and Daddy hear you. It's a really incredible story, how I got them. The older one, Felinity, which is a name I made up because she's—*(To cat carrier.)*—such a gorgeous, gorgeous girl—

(IRV's eyes get bigger and bigger in the course of her speech, horrified at what he's set in motion. He paces throughout, moves the cat carrier, and sneezes. Zap sound. Blackout. Lights come up on the RUSSIAN PLAY, as before. KONSTANTIN is now most of the way across the stage.)

(Zap sound. Blackout. Lights come up on the PERFORMANCE ART MONOLOGUE. MARSHA, seated with a glass of salty water in hand, is in the midst of gargling loudly.)

(Zap sound. Blackout. Lights come up on RICHARD III. Trying to get their last entrance right, RICHARD and

BUCKINGHAM again enter proudly. No trumpet flourish. RICHARD glares back into wings. The balalaika music from the RUSSIAN PLAY begins. Both react with disgust, RICHARD striding furiously toward the wings. BUCKINGHAM watches. The music is violently cut off. RICHARD returns and they try their entrance again. The phone rings. RICHARD leaps forward, grabs the phone out of the wastebasket, and hurls it into the wings. BUCKINGHAM smiles at this. Then both cringe as the zap sound is heard. Blackout.)

(Lights come up on the SOUTHERN PLAY. CAROLINE is still searching for the will. After a moment, EMMALINE from the ENGLISH MYSTERY enters the room from the other side, begins searching it as well, then notices CAROLINE. Both freeze and stare at each other. Zap sound. Blackout.)

(Lights come up on the PERFORMANCE ART MONOLOGUE. MARSHA is still holding her glass and gargling, walking around the room while she does so. She finally empties her mouth into the fishbowl. Zap sound. Blackout.)

(Lights come up on the AVANT-GARDE PLAY. The MAN is on the phone—a white, modern, push-button model, replacing the original black phone. The WOMAN is still knitting. The female corpse is lying where the male corpse lay in their previous scenes.)

WOMAN. Is it ringing?

MAN. Yes.

WOMAN. Good. *(Pause.)* How many rings is that?

MAN. Two hundred forty-one . . . two hundred forty-two . . .

WOMAN. I'm going to have something to say about the service here when we fill out the hotel questionnaire.

MAN. There is no questionnaire.

WOMAN. But that's why you're calling the front desk. To ask them to send one up. Or, if they don't have one, to kindly have one printed.

MAN. Unfortunately, they don't seem to be answering.

WOMAN. Typical.

MAN. I'm sure they're quite busy attending to the other guests.

WOMAN. *(She throws down her imaginary knitting needles in anger, stands, and notices the female corpse for the first time, eyeing it while distractedly delivering her line.)* But we're the other guests, too.

MAN. No, dear. We're ourselves. We can never be the others.

WOMAN. *(Abandoning the script, trying to get the MAN to notice the corpse.)* Well, he's not himself.

MAN. *(HE notices the corpse and begins improvising nervously.)* No, he's not. You're right. That's extremely rare, isn't it? To be one of the others and not oneself. The problem of identity is of course central to—the last portion of this play. And since I was just about to try on the corpse's clothes, to see if they fit, I now find myself wondering, as I'm sure you are as well—

(Sharp knock at the door. MAN and WOMAN freeze, confused. NORFOLK from RICHARD III, still in Shakespearean dress, calls out "Room service" and enters briskly, dragging the male corpse, which he exchanges for the female.)

NORFOLK. Compliments of the hotel.

(He exits swiftly, leaving MAN and WOMAN speechless. Pause.)

WOMAN. I suppose, as long as it doesn't appear on our bill.

(Zap sound. Blackout. Lights come up on the ENGLISH MYS-TERY. The male corpse remains in place. BEETON, REV. SMYTHE, and COL. HARDWICKE enter.)

BEETON. Good lord, it's Lady—Lady—Lady—*(He sees that the corpse is male and can't finish his line.)*

COL. HARDWICKE. Lady Denslow. Indeed it is. How death changes one, eh, Reverend?

REV. SMYTHE. *(Still angry, he speaks his line distastefully through clenched teeth.)* Lady Denslow was loved by all the village. *(He abandons the script and his English accent from here on.)* But she made the mistake of telling secrets! *(Faces wings.)* Just like that teenage twerp!

(All lines are improvised from this point on. COL. HARD-WICKE and BEETON maintain their accents.)

COL. HARDWICKE. Reverend—

REV. SMYTHE. Let both their souls burn for eternity in Hell!

(The others are stunned by this outburst. BEETON clears his throat, faces REV. SMYTHE, and tries to get him back on track.)

BEETON. Aren't you going to say a few words over her— *(Looks at corpse and corrects himself.)*—him— *(Corrects himself again.)*—her. You remember.

REV. SMYTHE. Yeah. Sure, I've got a few things to say. *(He bends down, stares at the corpse with hatred, and then yells.)* You better watch your back, lady, if you know what's good for you! *(He gives the corpse a kick.)* That's what I've got to say. *(Pause.)*

COL. HARDWICKE. Right. Jolly good. Well, now, I've a suggestion. Let's deduce the murderer's identity, shall we, which only takes a few pages, actually. Then we wrap this thing up—*(To REV. SMYTHE.)*—and you can scoot off to your anger management class. What do you chaps say to that?

REV. SMYTHE. What do we say? How about, "Why don't you shut your pompous trap, Colonel." The fearless military man, who can't face an audience without petting his good luck stuffed rabbit before every entrance!

(COL. HARDWICKE stares in shock at REV. SMYTHE. Pause. COL. HARDWICKE abruptly turns in military fashion and strides offstage.)

BEETON. Yes. Well. May I propose—

REV. SMYTHE. Oh, shut up, Jeremy!

(Zap sound. Blackout. Lights come up on the COMEDY. IRV paces nervously while talking to SAMMY. Women's clothes are strewn on the couch and floor, remaining in place through subsequent scenes.)

IRV. But I'm the one who got her thrown out! I can't just tell her to go live in Central Park.

SAMMY. Is she really so bad? Maybe you two—

IRV. Are you kidding? I'm through with women! I told you! *(He picks a dress up off a chair, flings it on the floor, and sits down.)* Her stuff's everywhere. She gave half my things to the Salvation Army when I was out. Her cats want to sleep on my head. The minute they showed up, my allergies came back. Next week she's got three kids coming home from boarding school for the whole summer. It's not gonna work! You gotta do something!

SAMMY. So tell her the truth, that it was all a game.

IRV. I can't do that! She thinks I'm a saint!

SAMMY. Saint Moe. *(Considers.)* Never heard of him.

IRV. Mel!

SAMMY. Mel. Him, I remember. Patron saint of vengeful writers.

IRV. Come on, think!

SAMMY. The thoughts would flow faster if you'd pour me a drink.

IRV. Coming up.

(IRV walks toward the whiskey bottle, remembers that it's

empty, makes a U-turn, and gestures to SAMMY to con-
tinue his lines.)

SAMMY. *(Uncertainly, miming drinking.)* Mmmmm. That
sure tastes good. Hey, I've got it!

IRV. Yeah?

SAMMY. Yeah. You convinced her you're a saint, right?

IRV. Right.

SAMMY. So now you do the same about her husband. Make
him look like Saint Max. They get back together, she moves
back with him, and you go back to being Irv Weinstein,
deeply flawed cheapskate.

IRV. Great! How do we do it?

SAMMY. How? *(A stuffed rabbit flies through the air and
lands in front of SAMMY. IRV looks toward the wings.
SAMMY picks up the rabbit and stares at it.)* How? . . . Well,
you . . . I'm sure there's . . . a perfectly rational . . .

*(Zap sound. Blackout. Lights come up on RICHARD III,
act 5, late in scene 3. RICHARD is alone.)*

RICHARD. The sun will not be seen to-day;
The sky doth frown and lower upon our army.

I would these dewy tears were from the ground.
Not shine to-day! Why, what is that to me
More than to Richmond? for the self-same heaven
That frowns on me looks sadly upon him.

*(NORFOLK enters, his shoe hooking one of the pieces of
women's clothing on the floor. He notices this just as he's
about to speak and labors to shake himself free with con-
temptuous fury.)*

NORFOLK. Arm, arm, my lord! The foe vaunts in the field.

RICHARD. Come, bustle, bustle; caparison my horse.
Call up Lord Stanley, bid him bring his power:
I will lead forth my soldiers to the plain—

*(The zap sound is heard but lights remain. RICHARD snarls
contemptuously at the audience, then turns to NORFOLK,
dropping his accent.)*

They're not going to let us finish. *(Pause.)* What about
my horse speech? *(To audience.)* What about my horse
speech!

*(The zap sound is repeated several times. Blackout. When lights
come up, the casts of both the SOUTHERN PLAY and the
RUSSIAN PLAY are onstage. REGINALD is reading the
will to AARON, CAROLINE, and LUKE, who are dis-
persed around the room. IRINA, NIKOLAI, and OLGA*

stand among them. All are surprised at this, but each group feels it's rightly onstage. All maintain accents except where indicated.)

REGINALD. "I testify that I am of sound mind and that this will was amended freely, neither under threat nor—"

OLGA. Perhaps you'd care to finish your reading elsewhere.

CAROLINE. Actually, you're interrupting an extremely crucial—

IRINA. We're interrupting?

REGINALD. We're trying to read a will here. If y'all don't mind—

IRINA. And we, may I point out, have a scene of considerable import to present as well.

LUKE. *(To IRINA.)* Say, you want to go out for a drink after?

(Snubbing him, IRINA turns her back on LUKE, who takes advantage of the chance and readies himself to experimentally poke both her buttocks at once. Before he can do so, the female corpse is thrown into the room. IRINA screams and moves out of LUKE's reach. Rehearsed shock from the Russian cast; mild interest from the SOUTHERN cast.)

NIKOLAI. Great-Grandfather!

IRINA. *(To wings.)* Great-Grand*father*!

(The male corpse is thrown into the room, next to the female. The SOUTHERN cast rolls eyes and shakes heads. NIKOLAI crouches over the male corpse and examines it.)

NIKOLAI. Dead! Throwing himself down the stairs. Why didn't he think of this decades ago?

REGINALD. *(To Russian cast, indicating female corpse.)* Yeah? So who's she?

OLGA. *(Disdainfully.)* She's certainly not one of ours. Probably a forgotten member of your bizarre ménage.

(Sound of cat yowling. AARON looks toward the wings.)

CAROLINE. I got a feeling that's the sound of your train, Aaron. *(Cat yowls again. AARON throws up his hands in disgust.)* Don't be late.

(AARON picks up his suitcase and stomps off. The zap sound is heard, but the lights stay on and actors remain where they are.)

REGINALD. *(Determined to continue.)* "To my son, Reginald—"

(IRV and AUDREY enter, IRV's line beginning offstage.)

IRV. Like I said to you before, Max is a great guy. I couldn't be happier for—

(IRV and AUDREY look around in shock. Both improvise.)

AUDREY. I didn't know I was . . . interrupting.

IRV. It's fine. Really. I was just having a little . . . get-together. To celebrate . . . the fact that . . . that—

(EMMALINE enters breathlessly, calling to an offstage BEETON.)

EMMALINE. Beeton! I know who the murderer is!

IRV. —that we know who the murderer is.

EMMALINE. It's not Clifford after all! And it's *not* Colonel Hardwicke!

CAROLINE. Hell, woman, I could've told you that.

(EMMALINE stamps her foot in frustration and bolts offstage.)

AUDREY. *(To IRV.)* I guess I'll just collect my things.

(She begins picking up clothing.)

REGINALD. "To my son, Reginald—"

(Zap sound. MAN and WOMAN enter, still in robes, and improvise.)

WOMAN. I wonder if perhaps we're in the wrong room.

MAN. It said 704 on the door. *(Indicating AUDREY picking up items.)* I told you the housecleaning staff would eventually show up.

WOMAN. *(She looks around the room, then at AUDREY.)* After you've finished changing the bed, would you please change the wallpaper? This pattern is so depressing. Oh, and we'd like fresh corpses, also. These are beginning to putrefy.

(AUDREY ignores her. Loud thunderclap.)

CAROLINE. *(Indicating thunder.)* Don't worry, it's not for us. It's for somebody else.

(Offstage we hear REV. SMYTHE growling in a fury. The stuffed rabbit flies onto the stage, followed by REV. SMYTHE, who jumps up and down on it. This elicits the polka music at high volume. IRV taps his foot on the floor, to no effect, then jumps up and down, looking toward the wings. The music continues. The zap sound is heard over and over. COL. HARDWICKE enters, sees the rabbit, and hurls himself at REV. SMYTHE. The stage goes dark.

Sounds of fighting and shouting, fading as the fight and the actors move offstage. Polka music plays on, then abruptly stops. Lights come up on the PERFORMANCE ART MONOLOGUE.)

MARSHA. Whoa. Chekhov meets WrestleMania. Of course, you expect opening night to be a little rough. But I hear there might be some talent scouts in the audience, which could actually be pretty important for me—

(IRINA enters, unseen by MARSHA, and starts singing softly.)

IRINA. "Twelve drummers drumming,
Eleven pipers piping,
Ten lords a-leaping—"

(MARSHA whirls around in a rage. She sticks her tongue out at IRINA, covers her ears, and yells her lines at the audience. IRINA continues singing "The Twelve Days of Christmas" at increasing volume.)

MARSHA. So like I'd really appreciate it if you'd let me do this next scene, without being interrupted, you know, 'cause I think it really shows off what I can do—

(Zap sound. Blackout. Pause.)

RICHARD. *(Offstage.)* A horse! A horse! My kingdom for a horse—*dammit*!

(Pause. Lights come up on the empty stage.)

CURTAIN

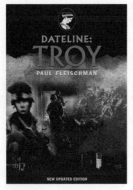
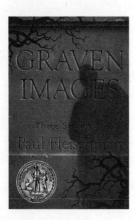